in an old castle wall, in a tiny, tiny hole . . .

there lived a little mouse called George.

and the Princess

CHRIS WORMELL

PUFFIN

Far, far away over the high, high mountains,

Now George, despite the sign above his hole,

was not dangerous or fierce at all.

In fact, he was rather timid . . .

and clumsy, too!

He was always trapping his tail in
the deckchair.

And he was hopeless at lighting fires.

And if he did get a fire going, he was bound to burn his cheese on toast.

Poor George was hopeless at most things.

But there was one small thing he *could* do . . .

actually, it was quite a big thing . . .

He could scare dragons!

Boo!

Well, he could scare *this* dragon.

Because *this* dragon was terrified of mice!

The princess turned out to be brilliant
at making cheese on toast.

She made extra-large portions, so George
could eat as much as he liked . . .

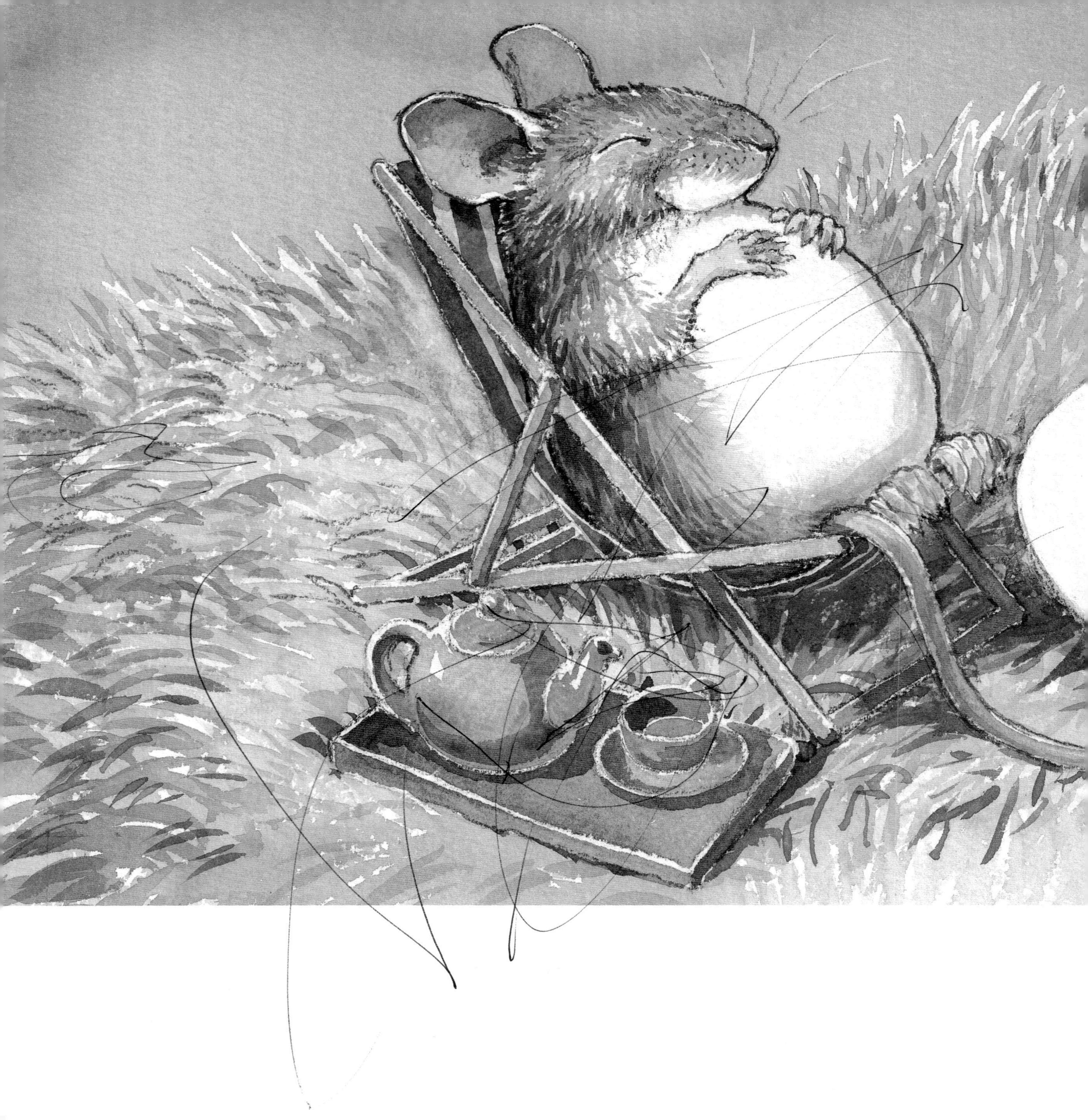

and he did!

**To Lucy, Laura and Chantelle**

PUFFIN BOOKS

UK | USA | Canada | Ireland | Australia
India | New Zealand | South Africa

Puffin Books is part of the Penguin Random House group of companies whose addresses can be found at global.penguinrandomhouse.com.

www.penguin.co.uk
www.puffin.co.uk
www.ladybird.co.uk

First published by Jonathan Cape 2007
Published by Red Fox 2008
This edition published 2018
001



Printed in China

A CIP catalogue record for this book is available from the British Library

ISBN: 978-0-241-36347-8

All correspondence to:
Puffin Books, Penguin Random House Children's
80 Strand, London WC2R 0RL